Connie Willis (signature)

CONNIE WILLIS

JACK

JACK

CONNIE WILLIS

Subterranean Press 2020

Signed, Limited Edition

ISBN
978-1-59606-963-3

Subterranean Press
PO Box 190106
Burton, MI 48519

subterraneanpress.com

Manufactured in the United States of America

THE NIGHT Jack joined our post, Vi was late. So was the Luftwaffe. The sirens still hadn't gone by eight o'clock.

"Perhaps our Violet's tired of the RAF and begun on the aircraft spotters," Morris said, "and they're so taken by her charms, they've forgotten to wind the sirens."

"You'd best watch out, then," Swales said, taking off his tin warden's hat. He'd just come back from patrol. We made room for him at the linoleum-covered table, moving our teacups and the litter of gas masks and pocket torches. Twickenham shuffled his papers into one pile next to his typewriter and went on typing.

Swales sat down and poured himself a cup of tea. "She'll set her cap for the ARP next," he said, reaching for the milk. Morris pushed it toward him. "And none of us will be safe." He grinned at me. "Especially the young ones, Jack."

"I'm safe," I said. "I'm being called up soon. Twickenham's the one who should be worrying."

Twickenham looked up from his typing at the sound of his name. "Worrying about what?" he asked, his hands poised over the keyboard.

"Our Violet setting her cap for you," Swales said. "Girls always go for poets."

"I'm a journalist, not a poet. What about Renfrew?" He nodded his head toward the cots in the other room.

"Renfrew!" Swales boomed, pushing his chair back and starting into the room.

"Shh," I said. "Don't wake him. He hasn't slept all week."

"You're right. It wouldn't be fair in his weakened condition." He sat back down. "And Morris is married. What about your son, Morris? He's a pilot, isn't he? Stationed in London?"

Morris shook his head. "Quincy's up at North Weald."

"Lucky, that," Swales said. "Looks as if that leaves you, Twickenham."

"Sorry," Twickenham said, typing. "She's not my type."

"She's not anyone's type, is she?" Swales said.

"The RAF's," Morris said, and we all fell silent, thinking of Vi and her bewildering popularity with the RAF pilots in and around London. She had pale eyelashes and colorless brown hair she put up in flat little pin curls while she was on duty, which was against regulations, though Mrs. Lucy didn't say anything to her about them. Vi was dumpy and rather stupid, and yet she was out constantly with one pilot after another, going to dances and parties.

"I still say she makes it all up," Swales said. "She buys all those things she says they give her herself, all those oranges and chocolate. She buys them on the black market."

"On a full-time's salary?" I said. We only made two pounds a week, and the things she brought home to the post—sweets and sherry and cigarettes—couldn't be bought on that. Vi shared them round freely, though liquor and cigarettes were against regulations as well. Mrs. Lucy didn't say anything about them, either.

She never reprimanded her wardens about anything, except being malicious about Vi, and we never gossiped in her presence. I wondered where she was. I hadn't seen her since I came in.

"Where's Mrs. Lucy?" I asked. "She's not late as well, is she?"

Morris nodded toward the pantry door. "She's in her office. Olmwood's replacement is here. She's filling him in."

Olmwood had been our best part-time, a huge out-of-work collier who could lift a house beam by himself, which was why Nelson, using his authority as district warden, had had him transferred to his own post.

"I hope the new man's not any good," Swales said. "Or Nelson will steal *him*."

"I saw Olmwood yesterday," Morris said. "He looked like Renfrew, only worse. He told me Nelson keeps them out the whole night patrolling and looking for incendiaries."

There was no point in that. You couldn't see where the incendiaries were falling from the street, and if there was an incident, nobody was anywhere to be found. Mrs. Lucy had assigned patrols at the beginning of the Blitz, but within a week she'd stopped them at midnight so we could get some sleep. Mrs. Lucy said she saw no point in our getting killed when everyone was already in bed anyway.

"Olmwood says Nelson makes them wear their gas masks the entire time they're on duty and holds stirrup-pump drills twice a shift," Morris said.

"Stirrup-pump drills!" Swales exploded. "How difficult does he think it is to learn to use one? Nelson's not getting me on his post, I don't care if Churchill himself signs the transfer papers."

The pantry door opened. Mrs. Lucy poked her head out. "It's half past eight. The spotter'd better go upstairs even if the sirens haven't gone," she said. "Who's on duty tonight?"

"Vi," I said, "but she hasn't come in yet."

"Oh, dear," she said. "Perhaps someone had better go look for her."

"I'll go," I said, and started pulling on my boots.

"Thank you, Jack," she said. She shut the door.

I stood up and tucked my pocket torch into my belt. I picked up my gas mask and slung it over my arm in case I ran into Nelson. The regulations said they were to be worn while patrolling, but Mrs. Lucy had realized early on that you couldn't see anything with them on. Which is why, I thought, she has the best post in the district, including Admiral Nelson's.

Mrs. Lucy opened the door again and leaned out for a moment. "She usually comes by underground. Sloane Square," she said. "Take care."

"Right," Swales said. "Vi might be lurking outside in the dark, waiting to pounce!" He grabbed Twickenham round the neck and hugged him to his chest.

"I'll be careful," I said, and went up the basement stairs and out onto the street.

I went the way Vi usually came from Sloane Square Station, but there was no one in the blacked-out streets except a girl hurrying to the underground station, carrying a blanket, a pillow, and a dress on a hanger.

I walked the rest of the way to the tube station with her to make sure she found her way, though it wasn't that dark. The nearly full moon was up, and there was a fire still burning down by the docks from the raid of the night before.

"Thanks awfully," the girl said, switching the hanger to her other hand so she could shake hands with me. She was much nicer looking than Vi, with blond, very curly hair. "I work for this old stewpot at John Lewis's, and she won't let me leave even a minute before closing, will she, even if the sirens have gone."

I waited outside the station for a few minutes and then walked up to the Brompton Road, thinking Vi might have come in at South Kensington instead, but I didn't see her, and she still wasn't at the post when I got back.

"We've a new theory for why the sirens haven't gone," Swales said. "We've decided our Vi's set her cap for the Luftwaffe, and they've surrendered."

"Where's Mrs. Lucy?" I asked.

"Still in with the new man," Twickenham said.

"I'd better tell Mrs. Lucy I couldn't find her," I said, and started for the pantry.

Halfway there the door opened, and Mrs. Lucy and the new man came out. He was scarcely a replacement for the burly Olmwood. He was not much older than I was, slightly built, hardly the sort to lift housebeams. His face was thin and rather pale, and I wondered if he was a student.

"This is our new part-time, Mr. Settle," Mrs. Lucy said. She pointed to each of us in turn. "Mr.

Morris, Mr. Twickenham, Mr. Swales, Mr. Harker."
She smiled at the part-time and then at me. "Mr.
Harker's name is Jack, too," she said. "I shall have to
work at keeping you straight."

"A pair of jacks," Swales said. "Not a bad hand."

The part-time smiled.

"Cots are in there if you'd like to have a liedown," Mrs. Lucy said, "and if the raids are close,
the coal cellar's reinforced. I'm afraid the rest of the
basement isn't, but I'm attempting to rectify that."
She waved the papers in her hand. "I've applied
to the district warden for reinforcing beams. Gas
masks are in there," she said, pointing at a wooden
chest, "batteries for the torches are in here"—she
pulled a drawer open—"and the duty roster's posted
on this wall." She pointed at the neat columns.
"Patrols here and watches here. As you can see,
Miss Westen has the first watch for tonight."

"She's still not here," Twickenham said, not
even pausing in his typing.

"I couldn't find her," I said.

"Oh, dear," she said. "I do hope she's all right.
Mr. Twickenham, would you mind terribly taking
Vi's watch?"

"I'll take it," Jack said. "Where do I go?"

"I'll show him," I said, starting for the stairs.

"No, wait," Mrs. Lucy said. "Mr. Settle, I hate to put you to work before you've even had a chance to become acquainted with everyone, and there really isn't any need to go up till after the sirens have gone. Come and sit down, both of you." She took the flowered cozy off the teapot. "Would you like a cup of tea, Mr. Settle?"

"No, thank you," he said.

She put the cozy back on and smiled at him. "You're from Yorkshire, Mr. Settle," she said as if we were all at a tea party. "Whereabouts?"

"Newcastle," he said politely.

"What brings you to London?" Morris said.

"The war," he said, still politely.

"Wanted to do your bit, eh?"

"Yes."

"That's what my son Quincy said. 'Dad,' he says, 'I want to do my bit for England. I'm going to be a pilot.' Downed twenty-one planes, he has, my Quincy," Morris told Jack, "and been shot down twice himself. Oh, he's had some scrapes, I could tell you, but it's all top secret."

Jack nodded.

There were times I wondered whether Morris, like Violet with her RAF pilots, had invented his son's exploits. Sometimes I even wondered if he had invented the son, though if that were the case, he might surely have made up a better name than Quincy.

"'Dad,' he says to me out of the blue, 'I've got to do my bit,' and he shows me his enlistment papers. You could've knocked me over with a feather. Not that he's not patriotic, you understand, but he'd had his little difficulties at school, sowed his wild oats, so to speak, and here he was, saying, 'Dad, I want to do my bit.'"

The sirens went, taking up one after the other. Mrs. Lucy said, "Ah, well, here they are now," as if the last guest had finally arrived at her tea party, and Jack stood up.

"If you'll just show me where the spotter's post is, Mr. Harker," he said.

"Jack," I said. "It's a name that should be easy for you to remember."

I took him upstairs to what had been Mrs. Lucy's cook's garret bedroom—unlike the street, a perfect place to watch for incendiaries. It was on the fourth floor, higher than most of the buildings on the street so one could see anything that fell on the roofs around. One could see the Thames, too, between the chimney pots, and in the other direction the searchlights in Hyde Park.

Mrs. Lucy had set a wing-backed chair by the window, from which the glass had been removed, and the narrow landing at the head of the stairs had been reinforced with heavy oak beams that even Olmwood couldn't have lifted.

"One ducks out here when the bombs get close," I said, shining the torch on the beams. "It'll be a swish and then a sort of rising whine." I led him into the bedroom. "If you see incendiaries, call out and try to mark exactly where they fall on the roofs." I showed him how to use the gunsight mounted on a wooden base that we used for a sextant and handed him the binoculars. "Anything else you need?" I asked.

"No," he said soberly. "Thank you."

I left him and went back downstairs. They were still discussing Violet.

"I'm really becoming worried about her," Mrs. Lucy said. One of the ack-ack guns started up, and there was the dull crump of bombs far away, and we all stopped to listen.

"ME 109's," Morris said. "They're coming in from the south again."

"I do hope she has the sense to get to a shelter," Mrs. Lucy said, and Vi burst in the door.

"Sorry I'm late," she said, setting a box tied with string on the table next to Twickenham's typewriter. She was out of breath and her face was suffused with color. "I know I'm supposed to be on watch, but Harry took me out to see his plane this afternoon, and I had a horrid time getting back." She heaved herself out of her coat and hung it over the back of Jack's chair. "You'll never believe what he's named it! The *Sweet Violet!*" She untied the string on the box. "We were so late we hadn't time for tea, and he said, 'You take this to your post and have a good tea, and I'll keep the jerries busy till you've finished,'" She reached in the box and lifted out a torte with sugar icing. "He's painted the name on the nose and put little violets in purple all round it," she said, setting it on the table. "One for every jerry he's shot down."

We stared at the cake. Eggs and sugar had been rationed since the beginning of the year, and they'd been in short supply even before that. I hadn't seen a fancy torte like this in over a year.

"It's raspberry filling," she said, slicing through the cake with a knife. "They hadn't any chocolate." She held the knife up, dripping jam. "Now, who wants some, then?"

"I do," I said. I had been hungry since the beginning of the war and ravenous since I'd joined the ARP, especially for sweets, and I had my piece eaten before she'd finished setting slices on Mrs. Lucy's Wedgwood plates and passing them round.

There was still a quarter left. "Who's upstairs taking my watch?" she said, sucking a bit of raspberry jam off her finger.

"The new part-time," I said. "I'll take it up to him."

She cut a slice and eased it off the knife and onto the plate. "What's he like?" she asked.

"He's from Yorkshire," Twickenham said, looking at Mrs. Lucy. "What did he do up there before the war?"

Mrs. Lucy looked at her cake, as if surprised that it was nearly eaten. "He didn't say," she said.

"I meant, is he handsome?" Vi said, putting a fork on the plate with the slice of cake. "Perhaps I should take it up to him myself."

"He's puny. Pale," Swales said, his mouth full of cake. "Looks as if he's got consumption."

"Nelson won't steal him anytime soon, that's certain," Morris said.

"Oh, well, then," Vi said, and handed the plate to me.

I took it and went upstairs, stopping on the second-floor landing to shift it to my left hand and switch on my pocket torch.

Jack was standing by the window, the binoculars dangling from his neck, looking out past the rooftops toward the river. The moon was up, reflecting whitely off the water like one of the German flares, lighting the bombers' way.

"Anything in our sector yet?" I said.

"No," he said, without turning round. "They're still to the east."

"I've brought you some raspberry cake," I said.

He turned and looked at me.

I held the cake out. "Violet's young man in the RAF sent it."

"No, thank you," he said. "I'm not fond of cake."

I looked at him with the same disbelief I had felt for Violet's name emblazoned on a Spitfire. "There's plenty," I said. "She brought a whole torte."

"I'm not hungry, thanks. You eat it."

"Are you sure? One can't get this sort of thing these days."

"I'm certain," he said, and turned back to the window.

I looked hesitantly at the slice of cake, guilty about my greed but hating to see it go to waste and still hungry. At the least I should stay up and keep him company.

"Violet's the warden whose watch you took, the one who was late," I said. I sat down on the floor, my back to the painted baseboard, and started to eat. "She's full-time. We've got five full-timers. Violet and I and Renfrew—you haven't met him yet, he was asleep. He's had rather a bad time. Can't sleep in the day—and Morris and Twickenham. And then there's Petersby. He's part-time like you."

He didn't turn around while I was talking or say anything, only continued looking out the window. A scattering of flares drifted down, lighting the room.

"They're a nice lot," I said, cutting a bite of cake with my fork. In the odd light from the flares the jam filling looked black. "Swales can be rather a nuisance with his teasing sometimes, and Twickenham will ask you all sorts of questions, but they're good men on an incident."

He turned around. "Questions?"

"For the post newspaper. Notice sheet, really, information on new sorts of bombs, ARP regulations, that sort of thing. All Twickenham's supposed to do is type it and send it round to the other posts, but I think he's always fancied himself an author, and now he's got his chance. He's named the notice sheet *Twickenham's Twitterings*, and he adds all sorts of things—drawings, news, gossip, interviews."

While I had been talking, the drone of engines overhead had been growing steadily louder. It passed, there was a sighing whoosh and then a whistle that turned into a whine.

"Stairs," I said, dropping my plate. I grabbed his arm and yanked him into the shelter of the landing. We crouched against the blast, my hands over my head, but nothing happened. The whine became a scream and then sounded suddenly farther off. I peeked round the reinforcing beam at the open window. Light flashed and then the crump came, at least three sectors away. "Lees," I said, going over to the window to see if I could tell exactly where it was. "High explosive bomb." Jack focused the binoculars where I was pointing.

I went out to the landing, cupped my hands, and shouted down the stairs, "HE. Lees." The planes were still too close to bother sitting down again. "Twickenham's done interviews with all the wardens," I said, leaning against the wall. "He'll want to know what you did before the war, why you became a warden, that sort of thing. He wrote up a piece on Vi last week."

Jack had lowered the binoculars and was watching where I had pointed. The fires didn't start right away with a high explosive bomb. It took a bit for the ruptured gas mains and scattered coal fires to catch. "What was she before the war?" he asked.

"Vi? A stenographer," I said. "And something of a wallflower, I should think. The war's been rather a blessing for our Vi."

"A blessing," Jack said, looking out at the high explosive in Lees. From where I was sitting, I couldn't see his face except in silhouette, and I couldn't tell whether he disapproved of the word or was merely bemused by it.

"I didn't mean a blessing exactly. One can scarcely call something as dreadful as this a blessing. But the war's given Vi a chance she wouldn't have had otherwise. Morris says without it she'd have died an old maid, and now she's got all sorts of beaus." A flare drifted down, white and then red. "Morris says the war's the best thing that ever happened to her."

"Morris," he said, as if he didn't know which one that was.

"Sandy hair, toothbrush mustache," I said. "His son's a pilot."

"Doing his bit," he said, and I could see his face clearly in the reddish light, but I still couldn't read his expression.

A stick of incendiaries came down over the river, glittering like sparklers, and fires sprang up everywhere.

∙
∙
∙
∙

THE NEXT night there was a bad incident off Old Church Street, two HEs. Mrs. Lucy sent Jack and me over to see if we could help. It was completely overcast, which was supposed to stop the Luftwaffe but obviously hadn't, and very dark. By the time we reached the King's Road, I had completely lost my bearings.

I knew the incident had to be close, though, because I could smell it. It wasn't truly a smell; it was a painful sharpness in the nose from the plaster dust and smoke and whatever explosive the Germans put in their bombs. It always made Vi sneeze.

I tried to make out landmarks, but all I could see was the slightly darker outline of a hill on my left. I thought blankly, We must be lost. There aren't any hills in Chelsea, and then realized it must be the incident.

"The first thing we do is find the incident officer," I told Jack. I looked round for the officer's blue light, but I couldn't see it. It must be behind the hill.

I scrabbled up it with Jack behind me, trying not to slip on the uncertain slope. The light was on the far side of another, lower hill, a ghostly bluish blur off to the left. "It's over there," I said. "We must report in. Nelson's likely to be the incident officer, and he's a stickler for procedure."

I started down, skidding on the broken bricks and plaster. "Be careful," I called back to Jack. "There are all sorts of jagged pieces of wood and glass."

"Jack," he said.

I turned around. He had stopped halfway down the hill and was looking up, as if he had heard something. I glanced up, afraid the bombers were coming back, but couldn't hear anything over the antiaircraft guns. Jack stood motionless, his head down now, looking at the rubble.

"What is it?" I said.

He didn't answer. He snatched his torch out of his pocket and swung it wildly round.

"You can't do that!" I shouted. "There's a blackout on!"

He snapped it off. "Go and find something to dig with," he said, and dropped to his knees. "There's someone alive under here."

He wrenched the bannister free and began stabbing into the rubble with its broken end.

I looked stupidly at him. "How do you know?"

He jabbed viciously at the mess. "Get a pickax. This stuff's hard as rock." He looked up at me impatiently. "Hurry!"

The incident officer was someone I didn't know. I was glad. Nelson would have refused to give me a pickax without the necessary authorization of duties. This officer, who was younger than me and broken out in spots under his powdering of brick dust, didn't have a pickax, but he gave me two shovels without any argument.

The dust and smoke were clearing a bit by the time I started back across the mounds, and a shower of flares drifted down over by the river, lighting everything in a fuzzy, overbright light like headlights in a fog. I could see Jack on his hands and knees halfway down the mound, stabbing with the bannister. He looked like he was murdering someone with a knife, plunging it in again and again.

Another shower of flares came down, much closer. I ducked and hurried across to Jack, offering him one of the shovels.

"That's no good," he said, waving it away.

"What's wrong? Can't you hear the voice anymore?"

He went on jabbing with the bannister. "What?" he said, and looked in the flare's dazzling light like he had no idea what I was talking about.

"The voice you heard," I said. "Has it stopped calling?"

"It's this stuff," he said. "There's no way to get a shovel into it. Did you bring any baskets?"

I hadn't, but farther down the mound I had seen a large tin saucepan. I fetched it for him and began digging. He was right, of course. I got one good shovelful and then struck an end of a floor joist and bent the blade of the shovel. I tried to get it under the joist so I could pry it upward, but it was wedged under a large section of beam farther on. I gave it up, broke off another of the bannisters, and got down beside Jack.

The beam was not the only thing holding the joist down. The rubble looked loose—bricks and chunks of plaster and pieces of wood—but it was as solid as cement. Swales, who showed up out of nowhere when we were three feet down, said, "It's

the clay. All London's built on it. Hard as statues."
He had brought two buckets with him and the news
that Nelson had shown up and had had a fight with
the spotty officer over whose incident it was.

"'It's *my* incident,' Nelson says, and gets out the
map to show him how this side of King's Road is in
his district," Swales said gleefully, "and the incident
officer says, '*Your* incident? Who wants the bloody
thing, I say,' he says."

Even with Swales helping, the going was so
slow, whoever was under there would probably have
suffocated or bled to death before we could get to
him. Jack didn't stop at all, even when the bombs
were directly overhead. He seemed to know exactly
where he was going, though none of us heard anything in those brief intervals of silence, and Jack
seemed scarcely to listen.

The bannister he was using broke off in the
iron-hard clay, and he took mine and kept digging.
A broken clock came up, and an egg cup. Morris
arrived. He had been evacuating people from two
streets over where a bomb had buried itself in the
middle of the street without exploding. Swales
told him the story of Nelson and the spotty young

officer and then went off to see what he could find out about the inhabitants of the house.

Jack came up out of the hole. "I need braces," he said. "The sides are collapsing."

I found some unbroken bed slats at the base of the mound. One of the slats was too long for the shaft. Jack sawed it halfway through and then broke it off.

Swales came back. "Nobody in the house," he shouted down the hole. "The colonel and Mrs. Godalming went to Surrey this morning." The all clear sounded, drowning out his words.

"Jack," Jack said from the hole.

"Jack," he said again, more urgently.

I leaned over the tunnel.

"What time is it?" he said.

"About five," I said. "The all clear just went."

"Is it getting light?"

"Not yet," I said. "Have you found anything?"

"Yes," he said. "Give us a hand."

I eased myself into the hole. I could understand his question; it was pitch-dark down here. I switched my torch on. It lit up our faces from beneath like spectres.

"In there," he said, and reached for a bannister just like the one he'd been digging with.

"Is he under a stairway?" I said, and the bannister clutched at his hand.

It only took a minute or two to get him out. Jack pulled on the arm I had mistaken for a bannister, and I scrabbled through the last few inches of plaster and clay to the little cave he was in, formed by an icebox and a door leaning against each other.

"Colonel Godalming?" I said, reaching for him.

He shook off my hand. "Where the bleeding hell have you people been?" he said. "Taking a tea break?"

He was in full evening dress, and his big mustache was covered with plaster dust. "What sort of country is this, leaving a man to dig himself out?" he shouted, brandishing a serving spoon full of plaster in Jack's face. "I could have dug all the way to China in the time it took you blighters to get me out!"

Hands came down into the hole and hoisted him up. "Blasted incompetents!" he yelled. We pushed on the seat of his elegant trousers. "Slackers, the lot of you! Couldn't find the nose in front of your own face!"

COLONEL GODALMING had in fact left for Surrey the day before but had decided to come back for his hunting rifle, in case of invasion. "Can't rely on the blasted Civil Defence to stop the jerries," he had said as I led him down to the ambulance.

It was starting to get light. The incident was smaller than I'd thought, not much more than two blocks square. What I had taken for a mound to the south was actually a squat office block, and beyond it the row houses hadn't even had their windows blown out.

The ambulance had pulled up as near as possible to the mound. I helped him over to it. "What's your name?" he said, ignoring the doors I'd opened. "I intend to report you to your superiors. And the other one. Practically pulled my arm out of its socket. Where's he got to?"

"He had to go to his day job," I said. As soon as we had Godalming out, Jack had switched on his pocket torch again to glance at his watch and said, "I've got to leave."

I told him I'd check him out with the incident officer and started to help Godalming down the mound. Now I was sorry I hadn't gone with him.

"Day job!" Godalming snorted. "Gone off to take a nap is more like it. Lazy slacker. Nearly breaks my arm and then goes off and leaves me to die. I'll have his job!"

"Without him we'd never even have found you," I said angrily. "He's the one who heard your cries for help."

"Cries for help!" the colonel said, going red in the face. "Cries for help! Why would I cry out to a lot of damned slackers?"

The ambulance driver got out of the car and came round to see what the delay was.

"Accused me of crying out like a damned coward!" he blustered to her. "I didn't make a sound. Knew it wouldn't do any good. Knew if I didn't dig myself out, I'd be there till Kingdom Come! Nearly had myself out, too, and then he comes along and accuses me of blubbering like a baby! It's monstrous, that's what it is! Monstrous!"

She took hold of his arm.

"What do you think you're doing, young woman? You should be at home instead of out running about in short skirts! It's indecent, that's what it is!"

She shoved him, still protesting, onto a bunk and covered him up with a blanket. I slammed the doors to, watched her off, and then made a circuit of the incident, looking for Swales and Morris. The rising sun appeared between two bands of cloud, reddening the mounds and glinting off a broken mirror.

I couldn't find either of them, so I reported in to Nelson, who was talking angrily on a field telephone and who nodded and waved me off when I tried to tell him about Jack, and then went back to the post.

Swales was already regaling Morris and Vi, who were eating breakfast, with an imitation of Colonel Godalming. Mrs. Lucy was still filling out papers, apparently the same form as when we'd left.

"Huge mustaches," Swales was saying, his hands two feet apart to illustrate their size, "like a walrus's, and tails, if you please. 'Oi siy, this is disgriceful!'" he sputtered, his right eye squinted shut with an imaginary monocle. "'Wot's the Impire coming to when a man cahn't even be rescued!'" He dropped into his natural voice. "I thought he was going to have our two Jacks court-martialed on the spot." He peered round me. "Where's Settle?"

"He had to go to his day job," I said.

"Just as well," he said, screwing the monocle back in. "The colonel looked like he was coming back with the Royal Lancers." He raised his arm, gripping an imaginary sword. "Charge!"

Vi tittered. Mrs. Lucy looked up and said, "Violet, make Jack some toast. Sit down, Jack. You look done in."

I took my helmet off and started to set it on the table. It was caked with plaster dust, so thick it was impossible to see the red W through it. I hung it on my chair and sat down.

Morris shoved a plate of kippers at me. "You never know what they're going to do when you get them out," he said. "Some of them fall all over you, sobbing, and some act like they're doing you a favor. I had one old woman acted all offended, claimed I made an improper advance when I was working her leg free."

Renfrew came in from the other room, wrapped in a blanket. He looked as bad as I thought I must, his face slack and gray with fatigue. "Where was the incident?" he asked anxiously.

"Just off Old Church Street. In Nelson's sector," I added to reassure him.

But he said nervously, "They're coming closer every night. Have you noticed that?"

"No, they aren't," Vi said. "We haven't had anything in our sector all week."

Renfrew ignored her. "First Gloucester Road and then Ixworth Place and now Old Church Street. It's as if they're circling, searching for something."

"London," Mrs. Lucy said briskly. "And if we don't enforce the blackout, they're likely to find it." She handed Morris a typed list. "Reported infractions from last night. Go round and reprimand them." She put her hand on Renfrew's shoulder. "Why don't you go have a nice liedown, Mr. Renfrew, while I cook you breakfast?"

"I'm not hungry," he said, but he let her lead him, clutching his blanket, back to the cot.

We watched Mrs. Lucy spread the blanket over him and then lean down and tuck it in around his shoulders, and then Swales said, "You know who this Godalming fellow reminds me of? A lady we rescued over in Gower Street," he said, yawning. "Hauled her out and asked her if her husband was in there with her. 'No,' she says, 'the bleedin' coward's at the front.'"

We all laughed.

"People like this colonel person don't deserve to be rescued," Vi said, spreading oleo on a slice of toast. "You should have left him there awhile and seen how he liked that."

"He was lucky they didn't leave him there altogether," Morris said. "The register had him in Surrey with his wife."

"Lucky he had such a loud voice," Swales said. He twirled the end of an enormous mustache. "Oi siy," he boomed. "Get me out of here im-meejutly, you slackers!"

But he said he didn't call out, I thought, and could hear Jack shouting over the din of the anti-aircraft guns, the drone of the planes, "There's someone under here."

Mrs. Lucy came back to the table. "I've applied for reinforcements for the post," she said, standing her papers on end and tamping them into an even stack. "Someone from the Town Hall will be coming to inspect in the next few days." She picked up two bottles of ale and an ashtray and carried them over to the dustbin.

"Applied for reinforcements?" Swales asked. "Why? Afraid Colonel Godalming'll be back with the heavy artillery?"

There was a loud banging on the door.

"Oi siy," Swales said. "Here he is now, and he's brought his hounds."

Mrs. Lucy opened the door. "Worse," Vi whispered, diving for the last bottle of ale. "It's Nelson." She passed the bottle to me under the table, and I passed it to Renfrew, who tucked it under his blanket.

"Mr. Nelson," Mrs. Lucy said as if she were delighted to see him, "do come in. And how are things over your way?"

"We took a beating last night," he said, glaring at us as though we were responsible.

"He's had a complaint from the colonel," Swales whispered to me. "You're done for, mate."

"Oh, I'm so sorry to hear that," Mrs. Lucy said. "Now, how may I help you?"

He pulled a folded paper from the pocket of his uniform and carefully opened it out. "This was forwarded to me from the City Engineer," he said. "All requests for material improvements are to be sent to the district warden, *not* over his head to the Town Hall."

"Oh, I'm so *glad*," Mrs. Lucy said, leading him into the pantry. "It is such a comfort to deal with someone one knows, rather than a faceless bureaucracy. If I had realized you were the proper person to appeal to, I should have contacted you *immediately*." She shut the door.

Renfrew took the ale bottle out from under his blanket and buried it in the dustbin. Violet began taking out her bobby pins.

"We'll never get our reinforcements now," Swales said. "Not with Adolf von Nelson in charge."

"Shh," Vi said, yanking at her snail-like curls. "You don't want him to hear you."

"Olmwood told me he makes them keep working at an incident, even when the bombs are right overhead. Thinks all the posts should do it."

"Shh!" Vi said.

"He's a bleeding Nazi!" Swales said, but he lowered his voice. "Got two of his wardens killed that way. You better not let him find out you and Jack are good at finding bodies, or you'll be out there dodging shrapnel, too."

Good at finding bodies. I thought of Jack, standing motionless, looking at the rubble and saying, "There's someone alive under here. Hurry."

"That's why Nelson steals from the other posts," Vi said, scooping her bobby pins off the table and into her haversack. "Because he does his own in." She pulled out a comb and began yanking it through her snarled curls.

The pantry door opened and Nelson and Mrs. Lucy came out, Nelson still holding the unfolded paper. She was still wearing her tea-party smile, but it was a bit thin. "I'm sure you can see it's unrealistic to expect nine people to huddle in a coal cellar for hours at a time," she said.

"There are people all over London 'huddling in coal cellars for hours at a time,' as you put it," Nelson said coldly, "who do not wish their Civil Defence funds spent on frivolities."

"I do not consider the safety of my wardens a frivolity," she said, "though it is clear to me that you do, as witnessed by your very poor record."

Nelson stared for a full minute at Mrs. Lucy, trying to think of a retort, and then turned on me. "Your uniform is a disgrace, warden," he said, and stomped out.

⋮

WHATEVER IT was Jack had used to find Colonel Godalming, it didn't work on incendiaries. He searched as haphazardly for them as the rest of us, Vi, who had been on spotter duty, shouting directions: "No, farther down Fulham Road. In the grocer's."

She had apparently been daydreaming about her pilots, instead of spotting. The incendiary was not in the grocer's but in the butcher's three doors down, and by the time Jack and I got to it, the meat locker was on fire. It wasn't hard to put out, there were no furniture or curtains to catch, and the cold kept the wooden shelves from catching, but the butcher was extravagantly grateful.

He insisted on wrapping up five pounds of lamb chops in white paper and thrusting them into Jack's arms.

"Did you really have to be at your day job so early, or were you only trying to escape the colonel?" I asked Jack on the way back to the post.

"Was he that bad?" he said, handing me the parcel of lamb chops.

"He nearly took my head off when I said you'd heard him shouting. Said he didn't call for help. Said he was digging himself out." The white butcher's paper was so bright, the Luftwaffe would think it was a searchlight. I tucked the parcel inside my overalls so it wouldn't show. "What sort of work is it, your day job?" I asked.

"War work," he said.

"Did they transfer you? Is that why you came to London?"

"No," he said. "I wanted to come." We turned into Mrs. Lucy's street. "Why did you join the ARP?"

"I'm waiting to be called up," I said, "so no one would hire me."

"And you wanted to do your bit."

"Yes," I said, wishing I could see his face.

"What about Mrs. Lucy? Why did she become a warden?"

"Mrs. Lucy?" I said blankly. The question had never even occurred to me. She was the best warden in London. It was her natural calling, and I'd thought of her as always having been one. "I've no idea," I said. "It's her house, she's a widow. Perhaps the Civil Defence commandeered it, and she had to become one. It's the tallest in the street." I tried to remember what Twickenham had written about her in his interview. "Before the war she had something to do with a church."

"A church," he said, and I wished again I could see his face. I couldn't tell in the dark whether he spoke in contempt or longing.

"She was a deaconess or something," I said. "What sort of war work is it? Munitions?"

"No," he said, and walked on ahead.

Mrs. Lucy met us at the door of the post. I gave her the package of lamb chops, and Jack went upstairs to replace Vi as spotter. Mrs. Lucy cooked the chops up immediately, running upstairs to the kitchen during a lull in the raids for salt and a jar of mint sauce, standing over the gas ring at the end

of the table and turning them for what seemed an eternity. They smelled wonderful.

Twickenham passed round newly run-off copies of *Twickenham's Twitterings.* "Something for you to read while you wait for your dinner," he said proudly.

The lead article was about the change in address of Sub-Post D, which had taken a partial hit that broke the water mains.

"Had Nelson refused them reinforcements, too?" Swales asked.

"Listen to this," Petersby said. He read aloud from the news sheet. "'The crime rate in London has risen twenty-eight percent since the beginning of the blackout.'"

"And no wonder," Vi said, coming down from upstairs. "You can't see your nose in front of your face at night, let alone someone lurking in an alley. I'm always afraid someone's going to jump out at me while I'm on patrol."

"All those houses standing empty, and half of London sleeping in the shelters," Swales said. "It's easy pickings. If I was a bad'un, I'd come straight to London."

"It's disgusting," Morris said indignantly. "The idea of someone taking advantage of there being a war to commit crimes."

"Oh, Mr. Morris, that reminds me. Your son telephoned," Mrs. Lucy said, cutting into a chop to see if it was done. Blood welled up. "He said he'd a surprise for you, and you were to come out to"—she switched the fork to her left hand and rummaged in her overall pocket till she found a slip of paper—"North Weald on Monday, I think. His commanding officer's made the necessary travel arrangements for you. I wrote it all down." She handed it to him and went back to turning the chops.

"A surprise?" Morris said, sounding worried. "He's not in trouble, is he? His commanding officer wants to see me?"

"I don't know. He didn't say what it was about. Only that he wanted you to come."

Vi went over to Mrs. Lucy and peered into the skillet. "I'm glad it was the butcher's and not the grocer's," she said. "Rutabagas wouldn't have cooked up half so nice."

Mrs. Lucy speared a chop, put it on a plate, and handed it to Vi. "Take this up to Jack," she said.

"He doesn't want any," Vi said. She took the plate and sat down at the table.

"Did he say why he didn't?" I asked.

She looked curiously at me. "I suppose he's not hungry," she said. "Or perhaps he doesn't like lamb chops."

"I do hope he's not in any trouble," Morris said, and it took me a minute to realize he was talking about his son. "He's not a bad boy, but he does things without thinking. Youthful high spirits, that's all it is."

"He didn't eat the cake either," I said. "Did he say why he didn't want the lamb chop?"

"If Mr. Settle doesn't want it, then take it to Mr. Renfrew," Mrs. Lucy said sharply. She snatched the plate away from Vi. "And don't let him tell you he's not hungry. He must eat. He's getting very run-down."

Vi sighed and stood up. Mrs. Lucy handed her back the plate, and she went into the other room.

"We all need to eat plenty of good food and get lots of sleep," Mrs. Lucy said reprovingly. "To keep our strength up."

"I've written an article about it in the *Twitterings*," Twickenham said, beaming. "It's known as 'walking death.' It's brought about by lack of sleep and poor nutrition, with the anxiety of the raids. The walking dead exhibit slowed reaction time and impaired judgment, which result in increased accidents on the job."

"Well, I won't have any walking dead among *my* wardens," Mrs. Lucy said, dishing up the rest of the chops. "As soon as you've had these, I want you all to go to bed."

The chops tasted even better than they had smelled. I ate mine, reading Twickenham's article on the walking dead. It said that loss of appetite was a common reaction to the raids. It also said that lack of sleep could cause compulsive behavior and odd fixations. "The walking dead may become convinced that they are being poisoned or that a friend or relative is a German agent. They may hallucinate, hearing voices, seeing visions, or believing fantastical things."

"He was in trouble at school, before the war, but he's steadied down since he joined up," Morris said. "I wonder what he's done."

AT THREE the next morning a land mine exploded in almost the same spot off Old Church Street as the HEs. Nelson sent Olmwood to ask for help, and Mrs. Lucy ordered Swales, Jack, and me to go with him.

"The mine didn't land more'n two houses away from the first crater," Olmwood said while we were getting on our gear. "The jerries couldn't have come closer if they'd been aiming at it."

"I know what they're aiming at," Renfrew said from the doorway. He looked terrible, pale and drawn as a ghost. "And I know why you've applied for reinforcements for the post. It's me, isn't it? They're after me."

"They're not after any of us," Mrs. Lucy said firmly. "They're two miles up. They're not aiming at anything."

"Why would Hitler want to bomb you more than the rest of us?" Swales said.

"I don't know." He sank down on one of the chairs and put his head in his hands. "I don't *know*. But they're after me. I can feel it."

Mrs. Lucy had sent Swales, Jack, and me to the incident because "you've been there before. You'll

know the terrain." But that was a fond hope. Since they explode above ground, land mines do considerably more damage then HEs. There was now a hill where the incident officer's tent had been, and three more beyond it, a mountain range in the middle of London. Swales started up the nearest peak to look for the incident officer's light.

"Jack, over here!" somebody called from the hill behind us, and both of us scrambled up a slope toward the voice.

A group of five men were halfway up the hill looking down into a hole.

"Jack!" the man yelled again. He was wearing a blue foreman's arm band, and he was looking straight past us at someone toiling up the slope with what looked like a stirrup pump. I thought, surely they're not trying to fight a fire down that shaft, and then saw it wasn't a pump. It was, in fact, an automobile jack, and the man with the blue arm band reached between us for it, lowered it down the hole, and scrambled in after it.

The rest of the rescue squad stood looking down into the blackness as if they could actually see something. After a while they began handing empty buckets down into the hole and pulling them out heaped full of broken bricks and pieces of splintered wood. None of them took any notice of us, even when Jack held out his hands to take one of the buckets.

"We're from Chelsea," I shouted to the foreman over the din of the planes and bombs. "What can we do to help?"

They went on bucket-brigading. A china teapot came up on the top of one load, covered with dust but not even chipped.

I tried again. "Who is it down there?"

"Two of 'em," the man nearest me said. He plucked the teapot off the heap and handed it to the man wearing a balaclava under his helmet. "Man and a woman."

"We're from Chelsea," I shouted over a burst of antiaircraft fire. "What do you want us to do?"

He took the teapot away from the man with the balaclava and handed it to me. "Take this down to the pavement with the other valuables."

It took me a long while to get down the slope, holding the teapot in one hand and the lid on with the other and trying to keep my footing among the broken bricks, and even longer to find any pavement. The land mine had heaved most of it up, and the street with it.

I finally found it, a square of unbroken pavement in front of a blown-out bakery, with the "valuables" neatly lined up against it: a radio, a boot, two serving spoons like the one Colonel Godalming had threatened me with, a lady's beaded evening bag. A rescue worker was standing guard next to them.

"Halt!" he said, stepping in front of them as I came up, holding a pocket torch or a gun. "No one's allowed inside the incident perimeter."

"I'm ARP," I said hastily. "Jack Harker. Chelsea." I held up the teapot. "They sent me down with this."

It was a torch. He flicked it on and off, an eye blink. "Sorry," he said. "We've had a good deal of looting recently." He took the teapot and placed it at the end of the line next to the evening bag. "Caught a man last week going through the pockets of the bodies laid out in the street waiting for the mortuary van. Terrible how some people will take advantage of a thing like this."

I went back up to where the rescue workers were digging. Jack was at the mouth of the shaft, hauling buckets up and handing them back. I got in line behind him.

"Have they found them yet?" I asked him as soon as there was a lull in the bombing.

"Quiet!" a voice shouted from the hole, and the man in the balaclava repeated, "Quiet, everyone! We must have absolute quiet!"

Everyone stopped working and listened. Jack had handed me a bucket full of bricks, and the handle cut into my hands. For a second there was absolute silence, and then the drone of a plane and the distant swish and crump of an HE.

"Don't worry," the voice from the hole shouted, "we're nearly there." The buckets began coming up out of the hole again.

I hadn't heard anything, but apparently down in the shaft they had, a voice or the sound of tapping, and I felt relieved, both that one of them at least was still alive, and that the diggers were on course. I'd been on an incident in October where we'd had to stop halfway down and sink a new shaft because the rubble kept distorting and displacing the sound. Even if the shaft was directly above the victim, it tended to go crooked in working past obstacles, and the only way to keep it straight was with frequent soundings. I thought of Jack digging for Colonel Godalming with the bannister. He hadn't taken any soundings at all. He had seemed to know exactly where he was going.

The men in the shaft called for the jack again, and Jack and I lowered it down to them. As the man below it reached up to take it, Jack stopped. He raised his head, as if he were listening.

"What is it?" I said. I couldn't hear anything but the ack-ack guns in Hyde Park. "Did you hear someone calling?"

"Where's the bloody jack?" the foreman shouted.

"It's too late," Jack said to me. "They're dead."

"Come along, get it down here," the foreman shouted. "We haven't got all day."

He handed the jack down.

"Quiet," the foreman shouted, and above us, like a ghostly echo, we could hear the balaclava call, "Quiet, please, everyone."

A church clock began to chime, and I could hear the balaclava say irritatedly, "We must have absolute quiet."

The clock chimed four and stopped, and there was a skittering sound of dirt falling on metal. Then silence, and a faint sound.

"Quiet!" the foreman called again, and there was another silence, and the sound again. A whimper. Or a moan. "We hear you," he shouted. "Don't be afraid."

"One of them's still alive," I said.

Jack didn't say anything.

"We just *heard* them," I said angrily.

Jack shook his head.

"We'll need lumber for bracing," the man in the balaclava said to Jack, and I expected him to tell him it was no use, but he went off immediately and came back dragging a white-painted bookcase.

It still had three books in it. I helped Jack and the balaclava knock the shelves out of the case and then took the books down to the store of "valuables." The guard was sitting on the pavement going through the beaded evening bag.

"Taking inventory," he said, scrambling up hastily. He jammed a lipstick and a handkerchief into the bag. "So's to make certain nothing gets stolen."

"I've brought you something to read," I said, and laid the books next to the teapot. *"Crime and Punishment."*

I toiled back up the hill and helped Jack lower the bookshelves down the shaft, and after a few minutes buckets began coming up again. We re-formed our scraggly bucket brigade, the balaclava at the head of it and me and then Jack at its end.

The all clear went. As soon as it wound down, the foreman took another sounding. This time we didn't hear anything, and when the buckets started again, I handed them to Jack without looking at him.

It began to get light in the east, a slow graying of the hills above us. Two of them, several stories high, stood where the row houses that had escaped the night before had been, and we were still in their shadow, though I could see the shaft now, with the end of one of the white bookshelves sticking up from it like a gravestone.

The buckets began to come more slowly.

"Put out your cigarettes!" the foreman called up, and we all stopped, trying to catch the smell of gas. If they were dead, as Jack had said, it was most likely gas leaking in from the broken mains that had killed them, and not internal injuries. The week before we had brought up a boy and his dog, not a scratch on them. The dog had barked and whimpered almost up to when we found them, and the ambulance driver said she thought they'd only been dead a few minutes.

I couldn't smell any gas, and after a minute the foreman said, excited, "I see them!"

The balaclava leaned over the shaft, his hands on his knees. "Are they alive?"

"Yes! Fetch an ambulance!"

The balaclava went leaping down the hill, skidding on broken bricks that skittered down in a minor avalanche.

I knelt over the shaft. "Will they need a stretcher?" I called down.

"No," the foreman said, and I knew by the sound of his voice they were dead.

"Both of them?" I said.

"Yes."

I stood up. "How did you know they were dead?" I said, turning to look at Jack. "How did—"

He wasn't there. I looked down the hill. The balaclava was nearly to the bottom—grabbing at a broken window sash to stop his headlong descent, his wake a smoky cloud of brick dust—but Jack was nowhere to be seen.

It was nearly dawn. I could see the gray hills and at the far end of them the warden and his "valuables." There was another rescue party on the third hill over, still digging. I could see Swales handing down a bucket.

"Give a hand here," the foreman said impatiently, and hoisted the jack up to me. I hauled it over to the side and then came back and helped the foreman out of the shaft. His hands were filthy, covered in reddish-brown mud.

"Was it the gas that killed them?" I asked, even though he was already pulling out a packet of cigarettes.

"No," he said, shaking a cigarette out and taking it between his teeth. He patted the front of his coverall, leaving red stains.

"How long have they been dead?" I asked.

He found his matches, struck one, and lit the cigarette. "Shortly after we last heard them, I should say," he said, and I thought, but they were already dead by then. And Jack knew it. "They've been dead at least two hours."

I looked at my watch. I read a little past six. "But the mine didn't kill them?"

He took the cigarette between his fingers and blew a long puff of smoke. When he put the cigarette back in his mouth, there was a red smear on it. "Loss of blood."

.
.
.

THE NEXT night the Luftwaffe was early. I hadn't gotten much sleep after the incident. Morris had fretted about his son the whole day, and Swales had teased Renfrew mercilessly. "Göring's found out about your spying," he said, "and now he's sent his Stukas after you."

I finally went up to the fourth floor and tried to sleep in the spotter's chair, but it was too light. The afternoon was cloudy, and the fires burning in the East End gave the sky a nasty reddish cast.

Someone had left a copy of *Twickenham's Twitterings* on the floor. I read the article on the walking dead again, and then, still unable to sleep, the rest of the news sheet. There was an account of Hitler's invasion of Transylvania, and a recipe for butterless strawberry tart, and the account of the crime rate. "London is currently the perfect place for the criminal element," Nelson was quoted as saying. "We must constantly be on the lookout for wrongdoing."

Below the recipe was a story about a Scottish terrier named Bonny Charlie who had barked and scrabbled wildly at the ruins of a collapsed house till wardens heeded his cries, dug down, and discovered two unharmed children.

I must have fallen asleep reading that, because the next thing I knew Morris was shaking me and telling me the sirens had gone. It was only five o'clock.

At half past we had an HE in our sector. It was just three blocks from the post, and the walls shook, and plaster rained down on Twickenham's typewriter and on Renfrew, lying awake in his cot.

"Frivolities, my foot," Mrs. Lucy muttered as we dived for our tin hats. "We need those reinforcing beams."

The part-times hadn't come on duty yet. Mrs. Lucy left Renfrew to send them on. We knew exactly where the incident was—Morris had been looking in that direction when it went—but we still had difficulty finding it. It was still evening, but by the time we had gone half a block, it was pitch-black.

The first time that had happened, I thought it was some sort of after-blindness from the blast, but it's only the brick and plaster dust from the collapsed buildings. It rises up in a haze that's darker than any blackout curtain, obscuring everything. When Mrs. Lucy set up shop on a stretch of sidewalk and switched on the blue incident light, it glowed spectrally in the man-made fog.

"Only two families still in the street," she said, holding the register up to the light. "The Kirkcuddy family and the Hodgsons."

"Are they an old couple?" Morris asked, appearing suddenly out of the fog.

She peered at the register. "Yes. Pensioners."

"I found them," he said in that flat voice that meant they were dead. "Blast."

"Oh, dear," she said. "The Kirkcuddys are a mother and two children. They've an Anderson shelter." She held the register closer to the blue light. "Everyone else has been using the tube shelter." She unfolded a map and showed us where the Kirkcuddys' backyard had been, but it was no help. We spent the next hour wandering blindly over the mounds, listening for sounds that were impossible to hear over the Luftwaffe's comments and the ack-ack's replies.

Petersby showed up a little past eight and Jack a few minutes later, and Mrs. Lucy set them to wandering in the fog, too.

"Over here," Jack shouted almost immediately, and my heart gave an odd jerk.

"Oh, good, he's heard them," Mrs. Lucy said. "Jack, go and find him."

"Over here," he called again, and I started off in the direction of his voice, almost afraid of what I would find, but I hadn't gone ten steps before I could hear it, too. A baby crying, and a hollow, echoing sound like someone banging a fist against tin.

"Don't stop," Vi shouted. She was kneeling next to Jack in a shallow crater. "Keep making noise.

We're coming." She looked up at me. "Tell Mrs. Lucy to ring the rescue squad."

I blundered my way back to Mrs. Lucy through the darkness. She had already rung up the rescue squad. She sent me to Sloane Square to make sure the rest of the inhabitants of the block were safely there.

The dust had lifted a little but not enough for me to see where I was going. I pitched off a curb into the street and tripped over a pile of debris and then a body. When I shone my torch on it, I saw it was the girl I had walked to the shelter two nights before.

She was sitting against the tiled entrance to the station, still holding a dress on a hanger in her limp hand. The old stewpot at John Lewis's never let her off even a minute before closing, and the Luftwaffe had been early. She had been killed by blast, or by flying glass. Her face and neck and hands were covered with tiny cuts, and glass crunched underfoot when I moved her legs together.

I went back to the incident and waited for the mortuary van and went with them to the shelter. It took me three hours to find the families on my list. By the time I got back to the incident, the rescue squad was five feet down.

"They're nearly there," Vi said, dumping a basket on the far side of the crater. "All that's coming up now is dirt and the occasional rosebush."

"Where's Jack?" I said.

"He went for a saw." She took the basket back and handed it to one of the rescue squad, who had to put his cigarette into his mouth to free his hands before he could take it. "There was a board, but they dug past it."

I leaned over the hole. I could hear the sound of banging but not the baby. "Are they still alive?"

She shook her head. "We haven't heard the baby for an hour or so. We keep calling, but there's no answer. We're afraid the banging may be something mechanical."

I wondered if they were dead, and Jack, knowing it, had not gone for a saw at all but off to that day job of his.

Swales came up. "Guess who's in hospital?" he said.

"Who?" Vi said.

"Olmwood. Nelson had his wardens out walking patrols during a raid, and he caught a piece of shrapnel from one of the ack-acks in the leg. Nearly took it off."

The rescue worker with the cigarette handed a heaping basket to Vi. She took it, staggering a little under the weight, and carried it off.

"You'd better not let Nelson see you working like that," Swales called after her, "or he'll have you transferred to his sector. Where's Morris?" he said, and went off, presumably to tell him and whoever else he could find about Olmwood.

Jack came up, carrying the saw.

"They don't need it," the rescue worker said, the cigarette dangling from the side of his mouth. "Mobile's here," he said, and went off for a cup of tea. Jack knelt and handed the saw down the hole.

"Are they still alive?" I asked.

Jack leaned over the hole, his hands clutching the edges. The banging was incredibly loud. It must have been deafening inside the Anderson. Jack stared into the hole as if he heard neither the banging nor any voice.

He stood up, still looking into the hole. "They're farther to the left," he said.

How can they be farther to the left? I thought. We can hear them. They're directly under us. "Are they alive?" I said.

"Yes."

Swales came back. "He's a spy, that's what he is," he said. "Hitler sent him here to kill off our best men one by one. I told you his name was Adolf von Nelson."

⋮

THE KIRKCUDDYS were farther to the left. The rescue squad had to widen the tunnel, cut the top of the Anderson open, and pry it back, like opening a can of tomatoes. It took till nine o'clock in the morning, but they were all alive.

Jack left sometime before it got light. I didn't see him go. Swales was telling me about Olmwood's injury, and when I turned around, Jack was gone.

"Has Jack told you where this job of his is that he has to leave so early for?" I asked Vi when I got back to the post.

She had propped a mirror against one of the gas masks and was putting her hair up in pin curls. "No," she said, dipping a comb in a glass of water and wetting a lock of her hair. "Jack, could you reach me my bobby pins? I've a date this afternoon, and I want to look my best."

I pushed the pins across to her. "What sort of job is it? Did Jack say?"

"No. Some sort of war work, I should think." She wound a lock of hair around her finger. "He's had ten kills. Four Stukas and six 109's."

I sat down next to Twickenham, who was typing up the incident report. "Have you interviewed Jack yet?"

"When would I have had time?" Twickenham asked. "We haven't had a quiet night since he came."

Renfrew shuffled in from the other room. He had a blanket wrapped round him Indian style and a bedspread over his shoulders. He looked terrible, pale and drawn as a ghost.

"Would you like some breakfast?" Vi asked, prying a pin open with her teeth.

He shook his head. "Did Nelson approve the reinforcements?"

"No," Twickenham said in spite of Vi's signaling him not to.

"You must tell Nelson it's an emergency," he said, hugging the blanket to him as if he were cold. "I know why they're after me. It was before the war. When Hitler invaded Czechoslovakia. I wrote a letter to the *Times*."

I was grateful Swales wasn't there. A letter to the *Times*.

"Come, now, why don't you go and lie down for a bit?" Vi said, securing a curl with a bobby pin as she stood up. "You're tired, that's all, and that's what's getting you so worried. They don't even get the *Times* over there."

She took his arm, and he went docilely with her into the other room. I heard him say, "I called him a lowland bully. In the letter." The person suffering from severe sleep loss may hallucinate, hearing voices, seeing visions, or believing fantastical things.

"Has he mentioned what sort of day job he has?" I asked Twickenham.

"Who?" he asked, still typing.

"Jack."

"No, but whatever it is, let's hope he's as good at it as he is at finding bodies." He stopped and peered at what he'd just typed. "This makes five, doesn't it?"

Vi came back. "And we'd best not let von Nelson find out about it," she said. She sat down and dipped the comb into the glass of water. "He'd take him like he took Olmwood, and we're already shorthanded, with Renfrew the way he is."

Mrs. Lucy came in carrying the incident light, disappeared into the pantry with it, and came out again carrying an application form. "Might I use the typewriter, Mr. Twickenham?" she asked.

He pulled his sheet of paper out of the typewriter and stood up. Mrs. Lucy sat down, rolled in the form, and began typing. "I've decided to apply directly to Civil Defence for reinforcements," she said.

"What sort of day job does Jack have?" I asked her.

"War work," she said. She pulled the application out, turned it over, rolled it back in. "Jack, would you mind taking this over to headquarters?"

"Works days," Vi said, making a pin curl on the back of her head. "Raids every night. When does he sleep?"

"I don't know," I said.

"He'd best be careful," she said. "Or he'll turn into one of the walking dead, like Renfrew."

Mrs. Lucy signed the application form, folded it in half, and gave it to me. I took it to Civil Defence headquarters and spent half a day trying to find the right office to give it to.

"It's not the correct form," the sixth girl said. "She needs to file an A-114, Exterior Improvements."

"It's not exterior," I said. "The post is applying for reinforcing beams for the cellar."

"Reinforcements are classified as exterior improvements," she said. She handed me the form, which looked identical to the one Mrs. Lucy had already filled out, and I left.

On the way out Nelson stopped me. I thought he was going to tell me my uniform was a disgrace again, but instead he pointed to my tin hat and demanded, "Why aren't you wearing a regulation helmet, warden? 'All ARP wardens shall wear a helmet with the letter W in red on the front,'" he quoted.

I took my hat off and looked at it. The red W had partly chipped away so that it looked like a V.

"What post are you?" he barked.

"Forty-eight. Chelsea," I said, and wondered if he expected me to salute.

"Mrs. Lucy is your warden," he said disgustedly, and I expected his next question to be what was I doing at Civil Defence, but instead he said, "I heard about Colonel Godalming. Your post has been having good luck locating casualties these last few raids."

"Yes, sir," was obviously the wrong answer, and "No, sir," would make him suspicious. "We found three people in an Anderson last night," I said. "One of the children had the wits to bang on the roof with a pair of pliers."

"I've heard that the person finding them is a new man, Settle." He sounded friendly, almost jovial. Like Hitler at Munich.

"Settle?" I said blankly. "Mrs. Lucy was the one who found the Anderson."

⋮

MORRIS'S SON Quincy's surprise was the Victoria Cross. "A medal," he said over and over. "Who'd have thought it, my Quincy with a medal? Fifteen planes he shot down."

It had been presented at a special ceremony at Quincy's commanding officer's headquarters, and the Duchess of York herself had been there. Morris had pinned the medal on Quincy himself.

"I wore my suit," he told us for the hundredth time. "In case he was in trouble I wanted to make a good impression, and a good thing, too. What would the Duchess of York have thought if I'd gone looking like this?"

He looked pretty bad. We all did. We'd had two breadbaskets of incendiaries, one right after the other, and Vi had been on watch. We had had to save the butcher's again, and a baker's two blocks farther down, and a thirteenth-century crucifix.

"I *told* him it went through the altar roof," Vi had said disgustedly when she and I finally got it out. "Your friend Jack couldn't find an incendiary if it fell on him."

"You told Jack the incendiary came down on the church?" I said, looking up at the carved wooden figure. The bottom of the cross was blackened, and Christ's nailed feet, as if he had been burnt at the stake instead of crucified.

"Yes," she said. "I even told him it was the altar." She looked back up the nave. "And he could have seen it as soon as he came into the church."

"What did he say? That it wasn't there?"

Vi was looking speculatively up at the roof. "It could have been caught in the rafters and come down after. It hardly matters, does it? We put it out. Come on, let's get back to the post," she said, shivering. "I'm freezing."

I was freezing, too. We were both sopping wet. The AFS had stormed up after we had the fire under control and sprayed everything in sight with icy water.

"Pinned it on myself, I did," Morris said. "The Duchess of York kissed him on both cheeks and said he was the pride of England." He had brought a bottle of wine to celebrate the Cross. He got Renfrew up and brought him to the table, draped in his blankets, and ordered Twickenham to put his typewriter away. Petersby brought in extra chairs, and Mrs. Lucy went upstairs to get her crystal.

"Only eight, I'm afraid," she said, coming back with the stemmed goblets in her blackened hands. "The Germans have broken the rest. Who's willing to make do with the tooth glass?"

"I don't care for any, thank you," Jack said. "I don't drink."

"What's that?" Morris said jovially. He had taken off his tin helmet, and below the white line it left, he looked like he was wearing blackface in a music-hall show. "You've got to toast my boy at least. Just imagine. My Quincy with a medal."

Mrs. Lucy rinsed out the porcelain tooth glass and handed it to Vi, who was pouring out the wine. They passed the goblets round. Jack took the tooth glass.

"To my son Quincy, the best pilot in the RAF!" Morris said, raising his goblet.

"May he shoot down the entire Luftwaffe!" Swales shouted. "And put an end to this bloody war!"

"So a man can get a decent night's sleep!" Renfrew said, and everyone laughed.

We drank. Jack raised his glass with the others, but when Vi took the bottle round again, he put his hand over the mouth of it.

"Just think of it," Morris said. "My son Quincy with a medal. He had his troubles in school, in with a bad lot, problems with the police. I worried about him, I did, wondered what he'd come to, and then this war comes along and here he is a hero."

"To heroes!" Petersby said.

We drank again, and Vi dribbled out the last of the wine into Morris's glass. "That's the lot, I'm afraid." She brightened. "I've a bottle of cherry cordial Charlie gave me."

Mrs. Lucy made a face. "Just a minute," she said, disappeared into the pantry, and came back with two cobwebbed bottles of port, which she poured out generously and a little sloppily.

"The presence of intoxicating beverages on post is strictly forbidden," she said. "A fine of five shillings will be imposed for a first offence, one pound for subsequent offences." She took out a pound note and laid it on the table. "I wonder what Nelson was before the war?"

"A monster," Vi said.

I looked across at Jack. He still had his hand over his glass.

"A headmaster," Swales said. "No, I've got it. An Inland Revenue collector!"

Everyone laughed.

"I was a horrid person before the war," Mrs. Lucy said.

Vi giggled.

"I was a deaconess, one of those dreadful women who arranges the flowers in the sanctuary and gets up jumble sales and bullies the rector. 'The Terror of the Churchwardens,' that's what I used to be. I was determined that they should put the hymnals front side out on the backs of the pews. Morris knows. He sang in the choir."

"It's true," Morris said. "She used to instruct the choir on the proper way to queue up."

I tried to imagine her as a stickler, as a petty tyrant like Nelson, and failed.

"Sometimes it takes something dreadful like a war for one to find one's proper job," she said, staring at her glass.

"To the war!" Swales said gaily.

"I'm not sure we should toast something so terrible as that," Twickenham said doubtfully.

"It isn't all that terrible," Vi said. "I mean, without it, we wouldn't all be here together, would we?"

"And you'd never have met all those pilots of yours, would you, Vi?" Swales said.

"There's nothing wrong with making the best of a bad job," Vi said, miffed.

"Some people do more than that," Swales said. "Some people take positive advantage of the war. Like Colonel Godalming. I had a word with one of the AFS volunteers. Seems the colonel didn't come back for his hunting rifle, after all." He leaned forward confidingly. "Seems he was having a bit on with a blond dancer from the Windmill. *Seems* his wife thought he was out shooting grouse in Surrey, and now she's asking all sorts of unpleasant questions."

"He's not the only one taking advantage," Morris said. "That night you got the Kirkcuddys out, Jack, I found an old couple killed by blast. I put them by the road for the mortuary van, and later I saw somebody over there, bending over the bodies, doing something to them. I thought, he must be straightening them out before the rigor sets in, but then it comes to me. He's robbing them. Dead bodies."

"And who's to say they were killed by blast?" Swales said. "Who's to say they weren't murdered? There's lot of bodies, aren't there, and nobody looks close at them. Who's to say they were all killed by the Germans?"

"How did we get onto this?" Petersby said. "We're supposed to be celebrating Quincy Morris's medal, not talking about murderers." He raised his glass. "To Quincy Morris!"

"And the RAF!" Vi said.

"To making the best of a bad job," Mrs. Lucy said.

"Hear, hear," Jack said softly, and raised his glass, but he still didn't drink.

⋮

JACK FOUND four people in the next three days. I did not hear any of them until well after we had started digging, and the last one, a fat woman in striped pyjamas and a pink hair net, I never did hear, though she said when we brought her up that she had "called and called between prayers."

Twickenham wrote it all up for the *Twitterings*, tossing out the article on Quincy Morris's medal and typing up a new master's. When Mrs. Lucy borrowed the typewriter to fill out the A-114, she said, "What's this?"

"My lead story," he said. "'Settle Finds Four in Rubble.'" He handed her the master's.

"'Jack Settle, the newest addition to Post Forty-eight,'" she read, "'located four air-raid victims last night. "I wanted to be useful," says the modest Mr. Settle when asked why he came to London from Yorkshire. And he's been useful since his very first night on the job when he—'" She handed it back to him. "Sorry. You can't print that. Nelson's been nosing about, asking questions. He's already taken one of my wardens and nearly got him killed. I won't let him have another."

"That's censorship!" Twickenham said, outraged.

"There's a war on," Mrs. Lucy said, "and we're shorthanded. I've relieved Mr. Renfrew of duty. He's going to stay with his sister in Birmingham. And I wouldn't let Nelson have another one of my wardens if we were overstaffed. He's already got Olmwood nearly killed."

She handed me the A-114 and asked me to take it to Civil Defence. I did. The girl I had spoken to wasn't there, and the girl who was said, "This is for *interior* improvements. You need to fill out a D-268."

"I did," I said, "and I was told that reinforcements qualified as exterior improvements."

"Only if they're on the outside." She handed me a D-268. "Sorry," she said apologetically. "I'd help you if I could, but my boss is a stickler for the correct forms."

"There's something else you can do for me," I said. "I was supposed to take one of our part-times a message at his day job, but I've lost the address. If you could look it up for me. Jack Settle? If not, I've got to go all the way back to Chelsea to get it."

She looked back over her shoulder and then said, "Wait a mo," and darted down the hall. She came back with a sheet of paper.

"Settle?" she said. "Post Forty-eight, Chelsea?"

"That's the one," I said. "I need his work address."

"He hasn't got one."

He had left the incident while we were still getting the fat woman out. It was starting to get light. We had a rope under her, and a makeshift winch, and he had abruptly handed his end to Swales and said, "I've got to leave for my day job."

"You're certain?" I said.

"I'm certain." She handed me the sheet of paper. It was Jack's approval for employment as a part-time warden, signed by Mrs. Lucy. The spaces for work and home addresses had been left blank. "This is all there was in the file," she said. "No work permit, no identity card, not even a ration card. We keep copies of all that, so he must not have a job."

I took the D-268 back to the post, but Mrs. Lucy wasn't there. "One of Nelson's wardens came round with a new regulation," Twickenham said, running off copies on the duplicating machine. "All wardens will be out on patrol unless on telephone or spotter duty. *All* wardens. She went off to give him what-for," he said, sounding pleased. He was apparently over his anger at her for censoring his story on Jack.

I picked up one of the still-wet copies of the news sheet. The lead story was about Hitler's invasion of Greece. He had put the article about Quincy Morris's medal down in the right-hand corner under a list of "What the War Has Done for Us." Number one was, "It's made us discover capabilities we didn't know we had."

"Mrs. Lucy called him a murderer," Twickenham said.

A murderer.

"What did you want to tell her?" Twickenham said.

That Jack doesn't have a job, I thought. Or a ration card. That he didn't put out the incendiary in the church even though Vi told him it had gone through the altar roof. That he knew the Anderson was farther to the left.

"It's still the wrong form," I said, taking out the D-268.

"That's easily remedied," he said. He rolled the application into the typewriter, typed for a few minutes, handed it back to me.

"Mrs. Lucy has to sign it," I said, and he snatched it back, whipped out a fountain pen, and signed her name.

"What were you before the war?" I asked. "A forger?"

"You'd be surprised." He handed the form back to me. "You look dreadful, Jack. Have you had any sleep this last week?"

"When would I have had the chance?"

"Why don't you lie down now while no one's here?" he said, reaching for my arm the way Vi had reached for Renfrew's. "I'll take the form back to Civil Defence for you."

I shook off his arm. "I'm all right."

I walked back to Civil Defence. The girl who had tried to find Jack's file wasn't there, and the first girl was. I was sorry I hadn't brought the A-114 along as well, but she scrutinized the form without comment and stamped the back. "It will take approximately six weeks to process," she said.

"Six weeks!" I said. "Hitler could have invaded the entire Empire by then."

"In that case, you'll very likely have to file a different form."

I didn't go back to the post. Mrs. Lucy would doubtless be back by the time I returned, but what could I say to her? I suspect Jack. Of what? Of not liking lamb chops and cake? Of having to leave early for work? Of rescuing children from the rubble?

He had said he had a job, and the girl couldn't find his work permit, but it took the Civil Defence six weeks to process a request for a few beams. It would probably take them till the end of the war to file the work permits. Or perhaps his had been in the file, and the girl had missed it. Loss of sleep can result in mistakes on the job. And odd fixations.

I walked to Sloane Square Station. There was no sign of where the young woman had been.

They had even swept the glass up. Her stewpot of a boss at John Lewis's never let her go till closing time, even if the sirens had gone, even if it was dark. She had had to hurry through the blacked-out streets all alone, carrying her dress for the next day on a hanger, listening to the guns and trying to make out how far off the planes were. If someone had been stalking her, she would never have heard him, never have seen him in the darkness. Whoever found her would think she had been killed by flying glass.

He doesn't eat, I would say to Mrs. Lucy. He didn't put out an incendiary in a church. He always leaves the incidents before dawn, even when we don't have the casualties up. The Luftwaffe is trying to kill me. It was a letter I wrote to the *Times*. The walking dead may hallucinate, hearing voices, seeing visions, or believing fantastical things.

The sirens went. I must have been standing there for hours, staring at the sidewalk. I went back to the post. Mrs. Lucy was there. "You look dreadful, Jack. How long's it been since you've slept?"

"I don't know," I said. "Where's Jack?"

"On watch," Mrs. Lucy said.

"You'd best be careful," Vi said, setting chocolates on a plate. "Or you'll turn into one of the walking dead. Would you like a sweet? Eddie gave them to me."

The telephone pipped. Mrs. Lucy answered it, spoke a minute, hung up. "Slaney needs help on an incident," she said. "They've asked for Jack."

⋮

SHE SENT both of us. We found the incident without any trouble. There was no dust cloud, no smell except from a fire burning off to one side. "This didn't just happen," I said. "It's a day old, at least."

I was wrong. It was two days old. The rescue squads had been working straight through, and there were still at least thirty people unaccounted for. Some of the rescue squad were digging half-heartedly halfway up a mound, but most of them were standing about, smoking and looking like they were casualties themselves. Jack went up to where the men were digging, shook his head, and set off across the mound.

"Heard you had a bodysniffer," one of the smokers said to me. "They've got one in Whitechapel, too. Crawls round the incident on his hands and knees, sniffing like a bloodhound. Yours do that?"

"No," I said.

"Over here," Jack said.

"Says he can read their minds, the one in Whitechapel does," he said, putting out his cigarette and taking up a pickax. He clambered up the slope to where Jack was already digging.

It was easy to see because of the fire, and fairly easy to dig, but halfway down we struck the massive headboard of a bed.

"We'll have to go in from the side," Jack said.

"The hell with that," the man who'd told me about the bodysniffer said. "How do you know somebody's down there? I don't hear anything."

Jack didn't answer him. He moved down the slope and began digging into its side.

"They've been in there two days," the man said. "They're dead and I'm not getting overtime." He flung down the pickax and stalked off to the mobile canteen. Jack didn't even notice he was gone.

He handed me baskets, and I emptied them, and occasionally Jack said, "Saw," or "Tin-snips," and I handed them to him. I was off getting the stretcher when he brought her out.

She was perhaps thirteen. She was wearing a white nightgown, or perhaps it only looked white because of the plaster dust. Jack's face was ghastly with it. He had picked her up in his arms, and she had fastened her arms about his neck and buried her face against his shoulder. They were both outlined by the fire.

I brought the stretcher up, and Jack knelt down and tried to lay her on it, but she would not let go of his neck. "It's all right," he said gently. "You're safe now."

He unclasped her hands and folded them on her chest. Her nightgown was streaked with dried blood, but it didn't seem to be hers. I wondered who else had been in there with her. "What's your name?" Jack said.

"Mina," she said. It was no more than a whisper.

"My name's Jack," he said. He nodded at me. "So's his. We're going to carry you down to the ambulance now. Don't be afraid. You're safe now."

The ambulance wasn't there yet. We laid the stretcher on the sidewalk, and I went over to the incident officer to see if it was on its way. Before I could get back, somebody shouted, "Here's another," and I went and helped dig out a hand that the foreman had found, and then the body all the blood had come from. When I looked down the hill, the girl was still lying there on the stretcher, and Jack was bending over it.

⋮

I WENT out to Whitechapel to see the bodysniffer the next day. He wasn't there. "He's a part-time," the post warden told me, clearing off a chair so I could sit down. The post was a mess, dirty clothes and dishes everywhere.

An old woman in a print wrapper was frying up kidneys in a skillet. "Works days in munitions out to Dorking," she said.

"How exactly is he able to locate the bodies?" I asked. "I heard—"

"That he reads their minds?" the woman said. She scraped the kidneys onto a plate and handed it to the post warden. "He's heard it, too, more's the pity, and it's gone straight to his head. 'I can feel them under here,' he says to the rescue squads, like he was Houdini or something, and points to where they're supposed to start digging."

"Then how does he find them?"

"Luck," the warden said.

"I think he smells 'em," the woman said. "That's why they call 'em bodysniffers."

The warden snorted. "Over the stink the jerries put in the bombs and the gas and all the rest of it?"

"If he were a—" I said, and didn't finish it. "If he had an acute sense of smell, perhaps he could smell the blood."

"You can't even smell the bodies when they've been dead a week," the warden said, his mouth full of kidneys. "He hears them screaming, same as us."

"He's got better hearing than us," the woman said, switching happily to his theory. "Most of us are half-deaf from the guns, and he isn't."

I hadn't been able to hear the fat woman in the pink hair net, although she'd said she had called for help. But Jack, just down from Yorkshire, where they hadn't been deafened by antiaircraft guns for weeks, could. There was nothing sinister about it. Some people had better hearing than others.

"We pulled an army colonel out last week who claimed he didn't cry out," I said.

"He's lying," the warden said, sawing at a kidney. "We had a nanny, two days ago, prim and proper as you please, swore the whole time we was getting her out, words to make a sailor blush, and then claimed she didn't. 'Unclean words have *never* crossed my lips and never will,' she says to me." He brandished his fork at me. "Your colonel cried out, all right. He just won't admit it."

"I didn't make a sound," Colonel Godalming had said, brandishing his serving spoon. "Knew it wouldn't do any good," and perhaps the warden was right, and it was only bluster. But he hadn't wanted his wife to know he was in London, to find out about the dancer at the Windmill. He had had good reason to keep silent, to try to dig himself out.

I went home and rang up a girl I knew in the ambulance service and asked her to find out where they had taken Mina. She rang me back in a few minutes with the answer, and I took the tube over to St. George's Hospital. The others had all cried out, or banged on the roof of the Anderson, except Mina. She had been so frightened when Jack got her out, she couldn't speak above a whisper, but that didn't mean she hadn't cried or whimpered.

"When you were buried last night, did you call for help?" I would ask her, and she would answer me in her mouse voice, "I called and called between prayers. Why?" And I would say, "It's nothing, an odd fixation brought on by lack of sleep. Jack spends his days in Dorking, at a munitions plant, and has exceptionally acute hearing." And there is no more truth to my theory than to Renfrew's belief that the raids were brought on by his letter to the *Times*.

St. George's had an entrance marked "Casualty Clearing Station." I asked the nursing sister behind the desk if I could see Mina.

"She was brought in last night. The James Street incident."

She looked at a penciled and crossed-over roster. "I don't show an admission by that name."

"I'm certain she was brought here," I said, twisting my head round to read the list. "There isn't another St. George's, is there?"

She shook her head and lifted up the roster to look at a second sheet.

"Here she is," she said, and I had heard the rescue squads use that tone of voice often enough to know what it meant, but that was impossible. She had been under that headboard. The blood on her nightgown hadn't even been hers.

"I'm so sorry," the sister said.

"When did she die?" I said.

"This morning," she said, checking the second list, which was much longer than the first.

"Did anyone else come to see her?"

"I don't know. I've just been on since eleven."

"What did she die of?"

She looked at me as if I were insane.

"What was the listed cause of death?" I said.

She had to find Mina's name on the roster again. "Shock due to loss of blood," she said, and I thanked her and went to find Jack.

⋮

HE FOUND me. I had gone back to the post and waited till everyone was asleep and Mrs. Lucy had gone upstairs and then sneaked into the pantry to look up Jack's address in Mrs. Lucy's files. It had not been there, as I had known it wouldn't. And if there had been an address, what would it have turned out to be when I went to find it? A gutted house? A mound of rubble?

I had gone to Sloane Square Station, knowing he wouldn't be there, but having no other place to look. He could have been anywhere. London was full of empty houses, bombed-out cellars, secret places to hide until it got dark. That was why he had come here.

"If I was a bad'un, I'd head straight for London," Swales had said. But the criminal element weren't the only ones who had come, drawn by the black-out and the easy pickings and the bodies. Drawn by the blood.

I stood there until it started to get dark, watching two boys scrabble in the gutter for sweets that had been blown out of a confectioner's front window, and then walked back to a doorway down the street from the post, where I could see the door, and waited. The sirens went. Swales left on patrol. Petersby went in. Morris came out, stopping to peer at the sky as if he were looking for his son Quincy's plane. Mrs. Lucy must not have managed to talk Nelson out of the patrols.

It got dark. The searchlights began to crisscross the sky, catching the silver of the barrage balloons. The planes started coming in from the east, a low hum. Vi hurried in, wearing high heels and carrying a box tied with string. Petersby and Twickenham left on patrol. Vi came out, fastening her helmet strap under her chin and eating something.

"I've been looking for you everywhere," Jack said.

I turned around. He had driven up in a lorry marked ATS. He had left the door open and the motor running. "I've got the beams," he said. "For reinforcing the post. The incident we were on last night, all these beams were lying on top, and I asked the owner of the house if I could buy them from him."

He gestured to the back of the lorry, where jagged ends of wood were sticking out. "Come along, then, we can get them up tonight if we hurry." He started toward the truck. "Where were you? I've looked everywhere for you."

"I went to St. George's Hospital," I said.

He stopped, his hand on the open door of the truck. "Mina's dead," I said, "but you knew that, didn't you?"

He didn't say anything.

"The nurse said she died of loss of blood," I said. A flare drifted down, lighting his face with a deadly whiteness. "I know what you are."

"If we hurry, we can get the reinforcements up before the raid starts," he said. He started to pull the door to.

I put my hand on it to keep him from closing it. "War work," I said bitterly. "What do you do, make sure you're alone in the tunnel with them or go to see them in hospital afterward?"

He let go of the door.

"Brilliant stroke, volunteering for the ARP," I said. "Nobody's going to suspect the noble air-raid warden, especially when he's so good at locating casualties. And if some of those casualties die later, if somebody's found dead on the street after a raid, well, it's only to be expected. There's a war on."

The drone overhead got suddenly louder, and a whole shower of flares came down. The searchlights wheeled, trying to find the planes. Jack took hold of my arm.

"Get down," he said, and tried to drag me into the doorway.

I shook his arm off. "I'd kill you if I could," I said. "But I can't, can I?" I waved my hand at the sky. "And neither can they. Your sort don't die, do they?"

There was a long swish, and the rising scream. "I *will* kill you, though," I shouted over it. "If you touch Vi or Mrs. Lucy."

"Mrs. Lucy," he said, and I couldn't tell if he said it with astonishment or contempt.

"Or Vi or any of the rest of them. I'll drive a stake through your heart or whatever it takes," I said, and the air fell apart.

There was a long sound like an enormous monster growling. It seemed to go on and on. I tried to put my hands over my ears, but I had to hang on to the road to keep from falling. The roar became a scream, and the sidewalk shook itself sharply, and I fell off.

"Are you all right?" Jack said.

I was sitting next to the lorry, which was on its side. The beams had spilled out the back. "Were we hit?" I said.

"No," he said, but I already knew that, and before he had finished pulling me to my feet, I was running toward the post that we couldn't see for the dust.

⋮

MRS. LUCY had told Nelson having everyone out on patrol would mean no one could be found in an emergency, but that was not true. They were all there within minutes, Swales and Morris and Violet, clattering up in her high heels, and Petersby. They ran up, one after the other, and then stopped and looked stupidly at the space that had been Mrs. Lucy's house, as if they couldn't make out what it was.

"Where's Renfrew?" Jack said.

"In Birmingham," Vi said.

"He wasn't here," I explained. "He's on sick leave." I peered through the smoke and dust, trying to see their faces. "Where's Twickenham?"

"Here," he said.

"Where's Mrs. Lucy?" I said.

"Over here," Jack said, and pointed down into the rubble.

We dug all night. Two different rescue squads came to help. They called down every half hour, but there was no answer. Vi borrowed a light from somewhere, draped a blue head scarf over it, and set up as incident officer. An ambulance came, sat awhile, left to go to another incident, came back. Nelson took over as incident officer, and Vi came back up to help. "Is she alive?" she asked.

"She'd better be," I said, looking at Jack.

It began to mist. The planes came over again, dropping flares and incendiaries, but no one stopped work. Twickenham's typewriter came up in the baskets, and one of Mrs. Lucy's wineglasses.

At around three Morris thought he heard something, and we stopped and called down, but there was no answer. The mist turned into a drizzle. At half past four I shouted to Mrs. Lucy, and she called back, from far underground, "I'm here."

"Are you all right?" I shouted.

"My leg's hurt. I think it's broken," she shouted, her voice calm. "I seem to be under the table."

"Don't worry," I shouted. "We're nearly there."

The drizzle turned the plaster dust into a slippery, disgusting mess. We had to brace the tunnel repeatedly and cover it with a tarpaulin, and then it was too dark to see to dig. Swales lay above us, holding a pocket torch over our heads so we could see. The all clear went.

"Jack!" Mrs. Lucy called up.

"Yes!" I shouted.

"Was that the all clear?"

"Yes," I shouted. "Don't worry. We'll have you out soon now."

"What time is it?"

It was too dark in the tunnel to see my watch. I made a guess. "A little after five."

"Is Jack there?"

"Yes."

"He mustn't stay," she said. "Tell him to go home."

The rain stopped, and it began to get light. Jack glanced vaguely up at the sky.

"Don't even think about it," I said. "You're not going anywhere." We ran into one and then another of the oak beams that had reinforced the landing on the fourth floor and had to saw through them. Swales reported that Morris had called Nelson "a bloody murderer." Vi brought us paper cups of tea.

We called down to Mrs. Lucy, but there wasn't any answer. "She's probably dozed off," Twickenham said, and the others nodded as if they believed him.

We could smell the gas long before we got to her, but Jack kept on digging, and like the others, I told myself that she was all right, that we would get to her in time.

She was not under the table after all, but under part of the pantry door. We had to call for a jack to get it off her. It took Morris a long time to come back with it, but it didn't matter. She was lying perfectly straight, her arms folded across her chest and her eyes closed as if she were asleep. Her left leg had been taken off at the knee. Jack knelt beside her and cradled her head.

"Keep your hands off her," I said.

I made Swales come down and help get her out. Vi and Twickenham put her on the stretcher. Petersby went for the ambulance. "She was never a horrid person, you know," Morris said. "Never."

It began to rain again, the sky so dark, it was impossible to tell whether the sun had come up yet or not. Swales brought a tarp to cover Mrs. Lucy.

Petersby came back. "The ambulance has gone off again," he said. "I've sent for the mortuary van, but they said they doubt they can be here before half past eight."

I looked at Jack. He was standing over the tarp, his hands slackly at his sides. He looked worse then Renfrew ever had, impossibly tired, his face gray with wet plaster dust. "We'll wait," I said.

"There's no point in all of us standing here in the rain for two hours," Morris said. "I'll wait here with the... I'll wait here. Jack"—he turned to him—"go and report to Nelson."

"I'll do it," Vi said. "Jack needs to get to his day job."

"Is she up?" Nelson said. He clambered over the fourth-floor beams to where we were standing. "Is she dead?" He glared at Morris and then at my hat, and I wondered if he were going to reprimand me for the condition of my uniform.

"Which of you found her?" he demanded.

I looked at Jack. "Settle did," I said. "He's a regular wonder. He's found six this week alone."

.
.
.

TWO DAYS after Mrs. Lucy's funeral, a memo came through from Civil Defence transferring Jack to Nelson's post, and I got my official notice to report for duty. I was sent to basic training and then on to Portsmouth. Vi sent me food packets, and Twickenham posted me copies of his *Twitterings*.

The post had relocated across the street from the butcher's in a house belonging to a Miss Arthur, who had subsequently joined the post. "Miss Arthur loves knitting and flower arranging and will make a valuable addition to our brave little band," Twickenham had written. Vi had got engaged to a pilot in the RAF. Hitler had bombed Birmingham. Jack, in Nelson's post now, had saved sixteen people in one week, a record for the ARP.

After two weeks I was shipped to North Africa, out of the reach of the mails. When I finally got Morris's letter, it was three months old. Jack had been killed while rescuing a child at an incident. A delayed-action bomb had fallen nearby, but "that bloody murderer Nelson" had refused to allow the rescue squad to evacuate. The DA had gone off, the tunnel Jack was working in had collapsed, and he'd been killed. They had gotten the child out, though, and she was unhurt except for a few cuts.

But he isn't dead, I thought. It's impossible to kill him. I had tried, but even betraying him to von Nelson hadn't worked, and he was still somewhere in London, hidden by the blackout and the noise of the bombs and the number of dead bodies, and who would notice a few more?

In January I helped take out a tank battalion at Tobruk. I killed nine Germans before I caught a piece of shrapnel. I was shipped to Gibraltar to hospital, where the rest of my mail caught up with me. Vi had gotten married, the raids had let up considerably, Jack had been awarded the George Cross posthumously.

In March I was sent back to hospital in England for surgery. It was near North Weald, where Morris's son Quincy was stationed. He came to see me after the surgery. He looked the very picture of an RAF pilot, firm-jawed, steely-eyed, rakish grin, not at all like a delinquent minor. He was flying nightly bombing missions over Germany, he told me, "giving Hitler a bit of our own back."

"I heard you're to get a medal," he said, looking at the wall above my head as if he expected to see violets painted there, nine of them, one for each kill.

I asked him about his father. He was fine, he told me. He'd been appointed Senior Warden. "I admire you ARP people," he said, "saving lives and all that."

He meant it. He was flying nightly bombing missions over Germany, reducing their cities to rubble, creating incidents for their air-raid wardens to scrabble through looking for dead children. I wondered if they had bodysniffers there, too, and if they were monsters like Jack.

"Dad wrote to me about your friend Jack," Quincy said. "It must have been rough, hearing so far away from home and all."

He looked genuinely sympathetic, and I supposed he was. He had shot down twenty-eight planes and killed who knows how many fat women in hair nets and thirteen-year-old girls, but no one had ever thought to call him a monster. The Duchess of York had called him the pride of England and kissed him on both cheeks.

"I went with Dad to Vi Westen's wedding," he said. "Pretty as a picture she was."

I thought of Vi, with her pin curls and her plain face. It was as though the war had transformed her into someone completely different, someone pretty and sought after.

"There were strawberries and two kinds of cake," he said. "One of the wardens—Tottenham?—read a poem in honor of the happy couple. Wrote it himself."

It was as if the war had transformed Twickenham as well, and Mrs. Lucy, who had been the terror of the churchwardens. What the War Has Done for Us. But it hadn't transformed them. All that was wanted was for someone to give Vi a bit of attention for all her latent sweetness to blossom. Every girl is pretty when she knows she's sought after.

Twickenham had always longed to be a writer. Nelson had always been a bully and a stickler, and Mrs. Lucy, in spite of what she said, had never been either. "Sometimes it takes something dreadful like a war for one to find one's proper job," she'd said.

Like Quincy, who had been, in spite of what Morris said, a bad boy, headed for a life of petty crime or worse, when the war came along. And suddenly his wildness and daring and "high spirits" were virtues, were just what was needed.

What the War Has Done for Us, Number Two. It has made jobs that didn't exist before. Like RAF pilot. Like post warden. Like bodysniffer.

"Did they find Jack's body?" I asked, though I knew the answer. No, Quincy would say, we couldn't find it, or there was nothing left.

"Didn't Dad tell you?" Quincy said with an anxious look at the transfusion bag hanging above the bed. "They had to dig past him to get to the little girl. It was pretty bad, Dad said. The blast from the DA had driven the leg of a chair straight through his chest."

So I had killed him after all. Nelson and Hitler and I.

"I shouldn't have told you that," Quincy said, watching the blood drip from the bag into my veins as if it were a bad sign. "I know he was a friend of yours. I wouldn't have told you only Dad said to tell you yours was the last name he said before he died. Just before the DA went up. 'Jack,' he said, like he knew what was going to happen, Dad said, and called out your name."

He didn't though, I thought. And "that bloody murderer Nelson" hadn't refused to evacuate him. Jack had just gone on working, oblivious to Nelson and the DA, stabbing at the rubble as though he were trying to murder it, calling out "saw" and "wire cutters" and "braces." Calling out "jack." Oblivious to everything except getting them out before the gas killed them, before they bled to death. Oblivious to everything but his job.

I had been wrong about why he had joined the ARP, about why he had come to London. He must have lived a terrible life up there in Yorkshire, full of darkness and self-hatred and killing. When the war came, when he began reading of people buried in the rubble, of rescue wardens searching blindly for them, it must have seemed a godsend. A blessing.

It wasn't, I think, that he was trying to atone for what he'd done, for what he was. It's impossible, at any rate. I had killed only ten people, counting Jack, and had helped rescue nearly twenty, but it doesn't cancel out. And I don't think that was what he wanted. What he had wanted was to be useful.

"Here's to making the best of a bad job," Mrs. Lucy had said, and that was all any of them had been doing: Swales with his jokes and gossip, and Twickenham, and Jack, and if they found friendship or love or atonement as well, it was no less than they deserved. And it was still a bad job.

"I should be going," Quincy said, looking worriedly at me. "You need your rest, and I need to be getting back to work. The German army's halfway to Cairo, and Yugoslavia's joined the Axis." He looked excited, happy. "You must rest and get well. We need you back in this war."

"I'm glad you came," I said.

"Yes, well, Dad wanted me to tell you that about Jack calling for you." He stood up. "Tough luck, your getting it in the neck like this." He slapped his flight cap against his leg. "I hate this war," he said, but he was lying.

"So do I," I said.

"They'll have you back killing jerries in no time," he said.

"Yes."

He put his cap on at a rakish angle and went off to bomb lecherous retired colonels and children and widows who had not yet managed to get reinforcing beams out of the Hamburg Civil Defence and paint violets on his plane. Doing his bit.

A sister brought in a tray. She had a large red cross sewn to the bib of her apron.

"No, thanks, I'm not hungry," I said.

"You must keep your strength up," she said. She set the tray beside the bed and went out.

"The war's been rather a blessing for our Vi," I had told Jack, and perhaps it was. But not for most people. Not for girls who worked at John Lewis's for old stewpots who never let them leave early even when the sirens had gone. Not for those people who discovered hidden capabilities for insanity or betrayal or bleeding to death. Or murder.

The sirens went. The nurse came in to check my transfusion and take the tray away. I lay there for a long time, watching the blood come down into my arm.

"Jack," I said, and didn't know who I called out to, or if I had made a sound.